27

CW00840253

Rotten Ralph

Join me on 2 ROTTEN adventures

First published in 1999 by BBC Worldwide Ltd
Woodlands, 80 Wood Lane, London W12 0TT

Original text by Erika Strobel
Additional text and adaptation by Glenn Dakin
Worldwide copyright © Italtoons UK Ltd 1999
Design by The Dirty Cat Company Design Partnership
copyright © BBC Worldwide Ltd 1999
Stills copyright © Italtoons UK Ltd 1999

Based on the television series produced by Italtoons UK Ltd
and Tooncan Productions Inc. Series copyright © Italtoons UK
Ltd and Tooncan Productions Inc. 1999. Television series inspired
by the original **Rotten Ralph** books, created by Jack Gantos
and Nicole Rubel.

ISBN 0 563 55650 1

Colour origination by Dot Gradations Ltd, Wickford
Printed and bound in Italy by Printer Trento S.r.l.

Purrrfect Pet
&
One of Nine Lives

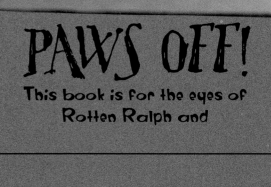

Purrrfect Pet

At school, Brenda and Buddy had their eyes on the prize!

It's all OURS, Buddy!

You'll be so proud of me when I win, Sarah! I'll show everyone what real talent is!

But Percy had his own ideas about that!

One of Nine Lives

Percy was coming across the road...

Hello, Ralph! You're looking your usual messy self today!

When suddenly he tripped...

OOOOF!

THUD!!

...right in the path of a bus!

Hey, Ralph, here's the answer — you gotta get Percy to save YOUR life...

Then you'll be EVEN!

Hey — that's a GREAT idea! All I need to do is come up with a plan...

All I have to do is FAKE an accident — like tripping on a bar of soap and nearly drowning...then Percy comes along and saves MY life!